THE CORN GROWS RIPE

"Simply but eloquently written and superbly illustrated."
—Chicago Sunday Tribune

"The whole has its special value in stimulating children to thinking in a new way about life-giving food, and also may linger in their minds to enrich their later thinking about world religion." *—New York Herald Tribune*

"Readers will discover here in the most natural and simplest way what a contemporary Indian culture is like. Jean Charlot's drawings, with their echo of ancient Mexican forms, are an admirable accompaniment to the text." *—Saturday Review*

THE CORN GROWS RIPE

THE

CORN

GROWS

RIPE

By DOROTHY RHOADS

ILLUSTRATED BY

JEAN CHARLOT

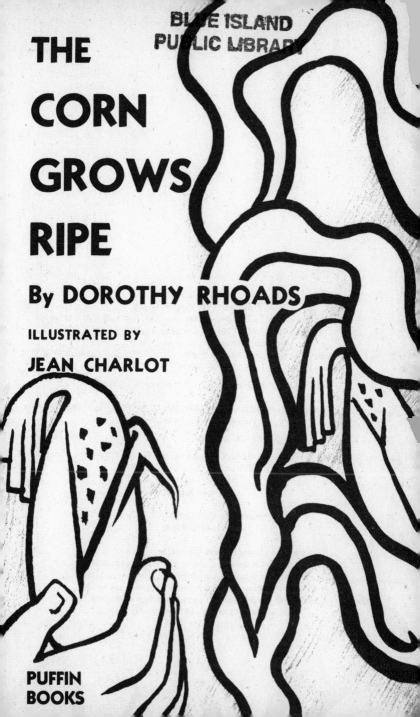

PUFFIN
BOOKS

PUFFIN BOOKS

Published by the Penguin Group

Penguin Putnam Inc., 375 Hudson Street, New York, New York 10014, U.S.A.

Penguin Books Ltd, 27 Wrights Lane, London W8 5TZ, England

Penguin Books Australia Ltd, Ringwood, Victoria, Australia

Penguin Books Canada Ltd, 10 Alcorn Avenue, Toronto, Ontario, Canada M4V 3B2

Penguin Books (N.Z.) Ltd, 182–190 Wairau Road, Auckland 10, New Zealand

Penguin Books Ltd, Registered Offices: Harmondsworth, Middlesex, England

First published in the United States of America by The Viking Press, 1956
Published in Puffin Books, 1993

30 29 28 27 26

Copyright © Dorothy Rhoads and Jean Charlot, 1956
Copyright renewed Dorothy Charlot, 1984
ISBN 0-14-036313-0
All rights reserved

Printed in the United States of America
Set in Times Roman

For my dearly loved sister

Frances,

whose devotion to and sympathetic

understanding of the Maya made this book possible

Contents

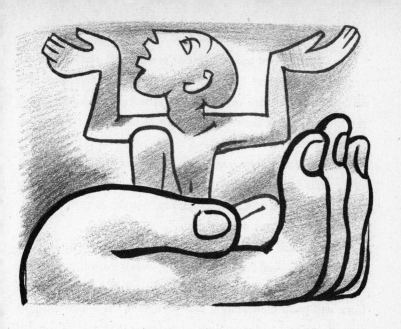

Foreword

There is an old Maya Indian folk tale which tells how man was created from corn.

In the beginning the Creator made the sky and the earth. He made the bush to cover the earth and all the animals and everything that grows. But there were no men.

"Something is missing," the Creator said. "Of what use are fruits and vegetables with no one to eat them? And what use are gods with no one to worship us? There should be men."

And the Creator took a bit of mud and made a man. He modeled him carefully, as men are formed today. But the man had no firmness or consistency. And when the rains came he dissolved.

The Creator tried again. He took some wood and carved out wooden people. And little wooden men and women filled the earth. But the wooden people were stiffnecked and hardhearted, and sawdust ran in their veins in place of blood. They could not worship gods.

So the Creator destroyed the wooden people. And He called all the gods and goddesses together in council to discuss what He could use to make man. Some suggested one thing, some another, but the Creator was not satisfied.

As they talked a bird flew into the council, carrying in its beak a seed of corn. And the Creator said, "Good! We will make man of corn. Corn will be the food man will eat during his lifetime. Corn will build man's blood and strengthen his bones and give him energy and understanding. It is fitting that man be created out of corn."

For more than two thousand years the Maya Indians of Central America have been eating corn. Always it has been their main food. Often during the centuries it has been their only food.

The Mayas' feeling for corn was almost a holy feeling. Their cornfields (called *milpas*), carved out of heavy forest, were their first altars. Making milpa (preparing the land) was a religious rite.

Their way of farming was based upon their climate—months of burning sun, followed by months of penetrating rains. At the beginning of the dry season man went into the forest, or bush, and cut down the trees and let them lie as they fell. And when the hot sun had thoroughly dried out the felled trees he burned them, clearing the land. At the beginning of the rainy season man sowed the seed, and when the rains were ending he harvested the ripe corn.

Before corn was discovered in what is Mexico today, the Mayas were a nomad people. They wandered through the bush in little groups, sleeping wherever night found them, and eating fruits and berries and game. And then, like a gift from their gods, came the knowledge of corn. The people turned from wandering and begán to settle on the land. A little village sprang up wherever the limestone crust of the earth had broken through to the underground water, forming a natural well. And around the villages in the bush were the cornfields.

Because it was important to know when to bush (fell trees) and when to burn and when to plant seed, the people began to take an interest in the seasons and in time. The wisest among them were set apart to do nothing but study the weather, and to learn the will of the gods who gave men weather. So priests began.

While the rest of the people farmed, the priests scanned the skies and studied the sun and moon and stars. And astronomy was born. As the science developed, lookouts were needed. And observatories were built, and little stone temples, to honor the gods. The temples rose higher as the people developed skill in building, and became more and more ornate as the people learned to paint and carve.

The priests, supported by the farmers, had nothing to do but study; they became great artists and scientists and scholars. And during the years a whole leisure class grew up, priests and secular lords and princes who devoted all their time to learning and the arts. They developed a system of writing and a calendar and became great mathematicians. The Mayas were the first people in the world to have the fixed point of zero in reckoning time. In astronomy they forecast eclipses and weather changes as surely as men do today.

Higher and higher above the bush rose the temples, built on great pyramid-foundations. Great cities grew out of the villages, and the rich civilization of the ancient Mayas matured, germinated from corn.

Today the priests and princes are gone. The ancient wisdom is forgotten. The great stone cities are only jungle-covered hills in the bush. But to the Maya Indians today, descendants of the ancient builders, corn is still the most important thing in the world. It is food and drink and money too, since with corn men buy cloth for clothing, and guns and medicine, and anything they need.

As their ancestors have done through the ages, men make milpa, cutting down bush and clearing the land by burning, and later sow the seed and harvest the ripe corn. Women grind the corn grains on their *metates* (stone grinders) and pat the mash into *tortillas* (round flat corncakes, which are baked like pancakes on a griddle) and mix *atole* (a drink made out of ground corn and water). And the gods who watch over men and shape the seasons send the sun and rain.

This story of a Maya Indian boy in Yucatán is also a story of corn. And since corn cannot grow without sun and rain, each in its season, it is a story too about weather.

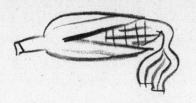

THE CORN GROWS RIPE

1. The Family

Dionisio opened his eyes slowly and blinked. Through the meshes of his hammock he looked about the room. The other hammocks —Mother's and Father's and Great-Grandmother's—were already tied up to the rafters for the day. Only his sister's small hammock of pink and white thread, though empty, swung beside his own.

Again he had overslept.

Always at night he made such fine resolutions. Tomorrow, he would tell himself, I will get up at dawn and help Father. I will bring in the firewood and water the goats before school. And always in the morning, his fine resolves forgotten, he lay clinging to sleep and his dream. He slept so soundly it was hard at times to wake up.

Through the open door the sun came in, quick and yellow, and with the sun the early daytime noises of the bush—the shrill clamor of the *chachalacas*, the soft cooing of doves, the liquid honey-sweet notes of the *pich*. The sounds stirred Dionisio's consciousness like soft lapping water. From the kitchen just outside came the sounds of Mother's and Great-Grandmother's voices and Concha's happy laughter.

Except for the kitchen, which was a separate room outside, the room in which the boy lay was the whole house. The sides were made of young trees cut from the bush, placed upright and fastened with vines. The floor was the earth. The roof was thatched with leaves of *guano* palm. The furniture too—what there was, a bench, a table, low stools, the altar at the end of the room—was made from trees cut from the bush. Everything Dionisio's family used and needed came from the forest that closed in around the small village, and closed out the outside world.

The bush dominated the thinking of the people. From the bush came life—corn, animals, healing herbs, wells with water. And from the bush came death. Not only the corn gods and rain gods lived in the bush. Evil winds, carrying sickness and bad fortune, lived there too, and witches and giants and all manner of supernatural beings that Great-Grandmother sometimes talked of around their fire at night. Buried in the bush were the ancient stone cities. Faraway on the bush the people first heard the rain at the end of the dry season, long before rain reached the village.

Louder and louder screamed the noisy chachalacas. Just outside and in the doorway hens scratched, cackling. A little yellow dog ran into the room and, poking a cold wet nose through the hammock mesh, softly licked the boy's cheek.

But Dionisio continued to swing in his hammock, half awake, half asleep.

"*Tee-gree, tee-gree, tee-gree,*" the pich bird sang, calling Dionisio by name.

He had been baptized Dionisio because that was the name of the saint on whose day he was born. But no one except the schoolmaster ever called him by anything but his pet name, Tigre—Jaguar.

"The name suits," Mother often said. "His skin is the wild honey color of the jaguar. And he is spirited and mischievous and curious."

"Yes. And lazy too," Great-Grandmother would add, "like all jaguars. And he thinks only of amusing himself. The boy is well named."

Remembering Great-Grandmother's words, Tigre sat up suddenly, fully awake. Ai! Here he lay as sleepy-eyed as Cat, today, when Father planned to go into the bush to start milpa.

He rolled up his hammock and tied it to the rafters with the others. At the end of the room he poured some water from the water jar into a basin and bathed. Then, scarcely stopping to dry himself, he put on a clean white shirt and the short white cotton trousers he wore for everyday, and hurried outside.

In the kitchen Mother and Great-Grandmother were shelling corn. Concha too had a pan in her lap, though she was only five.

She jumped up quickly, seeing Tigre, and the corn grains scattered, to disappear at once inside the hens and Dog.

"Here comes our privileged one," Great-Grandmother said, "our fine jaguar."

Tigre did not answer. He was getting used to Great-Grandmother's scolding. *Mamich* (little old grandmother) had lived with them ever since he could remember. She was as shriveled and dry as a dead leaf, and as brown. Her hair was white and all her teeth were gone. Tigre remembered other years when Mamich had been nothing but kindness to him. But lately, almost since the death of his three brothers, nothing he did seemed right.

"In my father's house," Great-Grandmother said, "my brothers got up with the daystar and brought in firewood. Boys learned early that they must work if they wish to eat."

Mother put down her pan and got up to give Tigre his breakfast—atole and some of yesterday's tortillas toasted on the iron griddle placed on three stones over the open fire on the floor.

"Let be, Mamich," Mother said gently. "He is only a child. He will be a man with man's work and man's worry soon enough."

"He is twelve," Great-Grandmother said. "Nearly a man. What kind of man will he be, doing only what he pleases?"

Tigre ate hungrily, stuffing down tortillas, gulping the hot atole. He tossed a tortilla to Dog, and Cat jumped down from the corncrib and wound herself, softly begging, about Tigre's legs.

"Father has gone for the wood. I watered the goats," Concha said, relating for Tigre the small happenings of the morning.

Tigre bent lower over his atole. His cheeks burned with shame.

Then Father came into the yard. He had a load of wood on his back, and he bent to unload it and pile it neatly against the side of the house.

Great-Grandmother began to grumble all over again. "When I was a girl no man would think of doing his son's work."

"He is only a cub," Father said. "He likes to dream and sport a little, like all young animals. He will sober in time."

"You too spoil him," Great-Grandmother said. "Because you lost three sons from fever, all within a week, is no reason to make a weakling of the fourth."

Father went into the house and took his gun and ax from the rafters. Mother handed him his hunting bag with his *calabaza,* a gourd bottle filled with water and some *masa,* dough made from boiled ground corn and water, wrapped in a banana leaf.

"Ready, Tigre?" Father said.

Ai! Tigre was ready. He crammed down another tortilla, grabbed his hat and hunting bag and slingshot, and hurried after Father. Dog, his little yellow tail curled happily over his back, ran after Tigre.

2. The Milpa

Tigre and Father and Dog passed quickly through the village and turned from the road into the bush.

Here the animals lived, deer and jaguar and wild pig, snakes and insects. Here were the ruins of the ancient stone-carved temples, now only tree-covered mounds. And here in the bush men made their cornfields, cutting down forest and clearing new land every few years.

The bush belonged to the gods, not to man. Men only borrowed it for a little because of their hunger, always asking the gods for permission. And after a few years they returned the land and made new clearings somewhere else. For two thousand years Tigre's people had used the land and returned it. And, always borrowing, never possessing or destroying, they had passed it on to their children as rich as it had been passed on to them.

They walked single file along the narrow trail, Father first, then Tigre, then Dog. Stones and roots of trees choked the pathway. Branches and thorns tore their clothing and scratched their cheeks.

Father had cut the trail when he chose the land for his milpa. It had not been used for some time, and already the bush was crowding back over the narrow opening, as it grew back over every open space—little-used trails, abandoned milpas, the ancient cities—until no one would know that a clearing had ever been there. The two seasons, months of sun alternating with months of rain, made for this fast-growing forest.

In the trees around them, birds sang full throated and hopped along the branches. Green vines and thin green tree snakes, still as vines, hung from the trees. New leaves from the recent rains crowded the bushes. Bright-colored flowers as gay as the tissue-paper decorations in the churches were caught among the green.

Tigre's spirits soared like birds' notes. Everything was beginning, he felt—a new year, a new milpa, the new dry season, new blossoms on the trees. Even the birds seemed to have new songs. In no time at all, it seemed, the trail ended, and they had reached Father's land.

It would be a fine cornfield. Large trees and palm trees grew thickly, which meant good black earth. And there was a hill with painted stones and broken bits of columns held in the vines and roots and branches of trees. Father had prayed and burned candles to San Diego so that he would choose his land well. And he had measured off his choice according to his needs—not more land than he could later clear. The bush gods who owned the trees punished greediness with sickness or bad fortune.

"Look, Father! One of the old temples," Tigre said.

"Yes," Father said. "Where there are stones there is humus. There is rich earth."

Tigre looked curiously at Father. To Father the temple was only good earth, or cut polished stones to be used in making a wall or in the floor of the village church. Did Father never wonder about the temples themselves or the men who had built them and worshiped at their ancient altars?

Ever since Tigre could remember, the temples had fascinated him. But to his many questions his parents gave the same unsatisfying answers. The buildings had been put up by "the old people" in the "good times." Beyond that no one knew.

Tigre sat down by one of the half-buried stones and began to scrape away the dirt with his knife. A warm rich red began to show beneath the dirt and then, as he scraped, the figure of an animal appeared. A jaguar! It was like an omen—as if the temple and land belonged to him.

He started to call to Father, but Father had already taken off his shirt and was briskly cutting one of the larger trees.

Tigre got up and with his *curva,* a short knife with a curved blade, began to cut, one by one, the vines and bushes that grew beneath a palm tree at the base of the mound. He sang as he worked, hitting fiercely at the bushes with fast, uneven strokes. But soon the song died away. The blows fell more slowly. The sun was hot, and his arms ached with the unaccustomed labor.

His back felt as if it were breaking. And for all his work he could not see that he had made much impression on the bush.

He sat down disconsolately on a stone and wiped the sweat from his face. Ai! It was not yet a cornfield. This tangle of trees and bush and vines must all be cut down and burned before it would be a field where seed could be sown.

Dog was scampering about over the mound as if he had not a care in the world. He had nosed out one of the great iguana lizards and chased it, barking fiercely, only to have the animal escape beneath a pile of stones.

Tigre fitted a pebble in his slingshot and aimed it idly at a yellow orchid in a tree above him. Back along the trail his quick eyes noted the wrinkled gray paper-like nest of bush hornets hanging from an *on* (avocado) tree. He fitted another stone and aimed it. The stone flew true, and Tigre laughed aloud as the hornets spilled out, confused and excitable as hens.

Fifty feet, he thought. Nearer sixty. And leaves and branches to deflect the stone. Ai! What things I could do if I had a gun! Deer and wild pig would be nothing. I could shoot a flying bird through the eye.

What Tigre wanted more than anything else in the world was a gun. Boys under fifteen were forbidden by law to take part in the communal hunts, but sometimes, when he and Father were alone in the bush, Father let Tigre take his gun to practice. "That way a boy learns," Father said. And already Tigre could hit his mark every time.

Father put down his ax and sat down beside Tigre. "Tired, son?" he asked.

Tigre nodded.

"A new clearing always means work. But it would be more work if we used the old field year after year. Weeds would spring up as thick and fast-growing as bush. It would take all our time to cut them—twelve months a year cutting weeds instead of one month felling trees. And weeds cause poor soil. Bush keeps out weeds and enriches the soil. So men use the land for a few years and return it to bush. Land gets weary too and needs rest, as men do," Father said.

He stood up and picked up his ax. "One stroke at a time. So many separate strokes and the work is done."

At noon they paused in their work and ate their tortillas. And Father made *pozole* by mixing, in a half-gourd cup, a little masa with water from his water gourd. Tigre hungrily gulped the nourishing milky beverage, and thought that never had the corn drink tasted so good.

Afterward Tigre rested for a little, lying under a tree, his hat over his eyes. When they stopped in the late afternoon only one small corner had been cleared in the large field.

The walk home seemed endless. Tigre stumbled on the trail. Silently he ate his tortillas and boiled black beans, with sauce of ground chili peppers. Mother took down his hammock and he fell asleep at once.

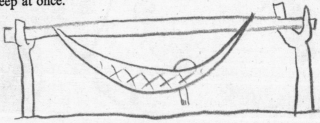

3. Trouble

The next morning Father woke Tigre before daylight. A candle burned dimly at one end of the room. The air was chill. Mother and Great-Grandmother were in the kitchen, making atole. Concha was still asleep.

Tigre shivered in the thin cotton clothes he had worn to bed the night before, his only protection from the cold. He ached all over. He could hardly move in his hammock without pain. He sat up, still half asleep, then fell back again with a groan.

"I feel bad," he said.

Father said nothing.

Tigre could hear him talking to Mother a moment later just outside the door. They were talking about him.

"Let him be," Mother said. "He worked too hard yesterday. He is only a boy. Tomorrow he will go with you again."

Then he heard Great-Grandmother's voice, strong with disapproval. "It would be better if you worried as much about his character as you do about his health. He is always ready to begin things. He must learn to finish them as well."

Tigre closed his eyes tightly. But try as he would he could not go back to sleep. About an hour later he got up. He bathed and dressed, every movement starting new aching in his back and limbs. I really must have hurt myself chopping down the trees, he thought.

Outside in the yard Mother was washing clothes under the *roble* tree. Great-Grandmother served Tigre his breakfast silently. He could not meet her eyes. "I will get in some wood before I go to school, Mamich," Tigre said. But Great-Grandmother would not answer.

After breakfast he went to the bush at the edge of the village. He made several trips and carried home enough wood for several days. He was ashamed to follow Father now.

All day as he sat in school there was the thought of Father between the lines of his lesson book—Father chopping the trees alone. At last Don Alfonso dismissed the class.

The other boys were going to the plaza to play ball. "Come on, Tigre," his friend Petuch called. But Tigre shook his head.

As soon as he entered the yard he knew that something had happened, for he could hear Mother crying. And as he reached the house he saw two strange guns leaning against the outside wall of the house. That meant strangers inside.

He should have known all along that something was going to happen, Tigre thought. All day he had had the feeling that bad luck would follow his failure to go with Father to the milpa. Perhaps the family would be punished in some way by one of the many minor bush gods who were so easy to offend. He hurried into the house.

Father lay in his hammock, silent and unmoving. Mother sat beside him, a pan of water in her lap, and Great-Grandmother was bending over Father, cutting away soiled, blood-soaked clothes. Two strange men sat in Mother's hammock.

They all looked up as Tigre entered.

"Father!" Tigre cried. "What has happened?"

Everyone began to talk at once.

"A tree fell on him," Mother said, and she began again to cry.

"He has offended the Balams (corn gods)," Great-Grandmother said.

"His leg is broken."

It had happened that morning. Father was chopping a tree and somehow it had fallen across his thigh. He had lain there for some time—how long he did not know—weak with pain.

After a little he had managed to move and get hold of his ax. And though the position was awkward he had cut away at the tree. Several times he had fainted, but when he came to he began again. Finally the tree was cut through and he was free. He rested for a little, then started to crawl, dragging himself along the trail. There the men had found him.

"It was only luck we chose that trail instead of another," the men said. "We were out hunting and—"

"We carried him in turn upon our backs."

Tigre could scarcely keep back the tears that welled up in him. "If I had been there," he cried, "it would not have happened!"

Great-Grandmother looked at him kindly. "He has offended the Kuilob Kaaxob (the gods of the bush) in some way," she said. "Or crossed the path of a Balam. If you had been there, who knows? Perhaps you too would have been harmed." There was no scolding in her voice.

"Do not blame yourself," Great-Grandmother continued. "Perhaps it was meant to be that you did not go."

She finished cutting away Father's clothes. She bathed the leg gently and put on a poultice of *anona* leaves and honey.

"He should have a bonesetter," one of the men said. "The bone is broken."

Tigre looked at Mother. There was no bonesetter in the village.

"In the head village there is a bonesetter who is also a medicine man," the man said.

Tigre nodded. "I will go," he said.

Mother was frightened. She began to cry again. "It is seventeen kilometers. In the bush. Something will happen to you too."

"Someone must go," the man said.

Great-Grandmother spoke up. "Good!" she said, as if it were all settled. "I will get your hunting bag ready, Tigre. I will put in a bottle of wild honey and a hen for the medicine man. Your clean clothes are ready. If you hurry you can get back by morning."

4. The Journey

Tigre put on his clean clothes slowly. Seventeen kilometers! Five hours! It would be dark long before he reached the village. He had never before been in the bush alone at night. At night all evil things walked the bush—evil winds and demons and strange monsters, animals that were not animals but witches who had taken animal forms.

But he said again, as if to reassure himself, "I will go."

Great-Grandmother handed him his hat and hunting bag. "There is masa and a calabash of water," she said, "and the hen and honey for the medicine man. Go with God."

As Tigre walked through the village, Dog running at his side, he thought that never had the village seemed so pleasant. It was clean and safe and friendly. He looked at it almost as if he were seeing it for the first time. Children hung over the walls and called to him. Men and women appeared in the doorways of the houses to wave good-by. All had heard of Father's accident and knew of Tigre's errand.

"Good journey," they called. "Walk with God."

He came to the end of the street and stopped before the pair of large wooden crosses that guarded the entrance to the village. These were the images of Holy Cross, a very ancient Maya *santo,* and the patron of the village. When Tigre passed beyond those crosses he passed beyond his own santo's protection.

Inside the bush the pale half-light of late afternoon had settled. The bright morning flowers were closing. A last bird hopped along a branch above him, sang a measure of evensong, and was still. Tigre walked as fast as he could, to put as much of the journey as possible behind him before night.

Darkness came suddenly. Tigre had never known such blackness. It closed over the bush like the wings of some enormous bird of evil. Even the stars were shut out by the trees. He shivered. With trembling fingers he lit his stick of pitch pine.

It gave almost no light at all. The feeble gleam on the trail before him seemed but to intensify the shadows all around. Anything could creep up on me from among those black shadows, he thought. The light only pointed him out to watching spirits who otherwise might have missed him in the dark. Whisperings and small stirrings sounded all around him.

This was the same bush through which he had passed with Father to the milpa, but now it was utterly strange. Everything about it was hostile. He felt small and terribly alone. He began to talk aloud to Dog, and the sound of his voice gave him courage.

"It is only some animal," he said. "A cow or a deer—that rustling noise. Do not be afraid."

Tigre said, "If I had a gun I would not be afraid of anything. When I have my gun a journey such as this will be nothing."

Dog kept close on his heels. Now and then he barked sharply or growled, and the sounds set the boy's heart to thumping.

In the darkness the branches that caught Tigre's clothing were clutching fingers. The tree roots that arched the trail were demons to trip him as he passed. Vines dropping from trees brushed his cheeks, and his thoughts flew to snakes. He remembered a story Great-Grandmother told about the Snake Witch. Thin as a pencil, she was, and she dropped on men from the trees and stopped up their nostrils. He remembered other stories —of the giant Juan who walked along the trails beating on a silver drum and catching children to eat; of the Palm-Leaf-Mat Witch who flew through the trees with wings of palm mats that rattled in the wind, and who hated children; of the Xtabai, as evil as they were beautiful, who lived in *ceiba* trees and bewitched men.

Suddenly Dog whined, a thin, eerie cry. A branch snapped, and Tigre began to run. He ran and ran, tripping and stumbling on the trail. Then he stopped, and in the sudden stillness his breathing seemed to stop too, and the pounding of his heart sounded like drumbeats.

"If it were nine o'clock in the morning instead of nine at night," he said to Dog, "we would not be afraid. Yet evil things walk in the light too." And the thought of Father urged him forward.

Ahead of him a ceiba tree stretched monstrous armlike branches across his path, and again he stopped. But he made himself go forward. He passed the tree, eyes on the ground, and nothing happened. A high whistling sounded in a tree above him, but quickly he identified the sound. It was one of the night birds.

When he reached the head village his clothes were wet with perspiration. "We are here," he said to Dog. "Nothing has harmed us after all."

He passed through the silent streets like a shadow. On either side of the road the gray rounded houses lay huddled like great sleeping pigs beneath the stars. In none of them did a light show. Tigre knocked at several houses before a woman's voice answered. He heard her say, "It is a boy. Perhaps he is in trouble." And a man opened the door and gave him directions to the bonesetter's house.

The medicine man got ready quickly. His wife filled his hunting bag and put in his calabash and masa, his medicines and remedies and divination stone.

The journey back was nothing, though Tigre could scarcely keep his eyes from closing and even Dog lagged behind. The trail was only a trail. The bush was only bush.

The white mist of early morning was rising from the ground

when they reached his village. Great-Grandmother met them at the door. She smiled at Tigre. Father was sleeping, she said. He had slept most of the night.

"Go to your hammock," Great-Grandmother told Tigre. "Do not worry. Everything will be all right."

5. Bushing Milpa

For several days the medicine man remained with the family. He set the broken bone and put a splint on Father's leg. He spent hours looking into his divination stone and making intricate counts with grains of corn to find out the cause of the accident.

"It is true," he said at last to the anxious family. "You have offended the corn gods. It will take a long time, but I see recovery in the stone. When the corn is in tassel you will be well again."

"Not until harvest time?" Father said and looked with dismay at Mother. "Who is to bush and burn and plant the milpa? Who is to bring the corn to tassel?"

"I will make milpa, Father," Tigre said.

The others turned toward him quickly.

"But you cannot do it alone, son," Mother said. "Perhaps your uncle, Pedro Paat, will come to help us. And another year, when Father is better, Father can return the work."

"There is no need," Tigre said. "I will make our cornfield. I will finish bushing. I will burn."

He could feel them all looking at him, Father and Mother with anxious glances, Great-Grandmother with her small black eyes hard and piercing.

Great-Grandmother seemed to read his thoughts. "Good!" she said. "Tigre will make our milpa. We can always depend on our men in *this* family."

Now the days began to drag for Tigre. In the morning he got up when Mother and Great-Grandmother did and dressed by candlelight. While Mother prepared atole he brought in wood for the day, and as soon as he had eaten he started with Dog to the milpa.

Mother had worried about his schoolwork. What if he failed, she said, when the government examiners came? And there would be not only the disgrace but the fines to pay as well. For the government imposed heavy penalties on parents who had illiterate children.

When Tigre asked the schoolmaster for permission to be absent from class, Don Alfonso not only consented but offered to help Tigre with his lessons.

"Come to my house in the evenings," he said. "It will not be easy, Dionisio. But there is no reason why you should not make milpa and pass your school examinations too."

At first Tigre worked fiercely, grim with purpose. But as day followed day and he seemed to make no impression on the forest, and for all his labor the standing trees stretched out, he was near despair.

"I cannot do it," he told Dog. "It is too much. I cannot do it and my schoolwork too."

And then, "Would Father stop?" he asked himself. And he thought how many times his father must have been weary too but kept on, so that Tigre and Mother and the others might have food. And he lifted the heavy ax with new determination.

"If we are even to eat now," he said to Dog, "it depends on me."

The hours stretched into days, days into weeks, and still he cut the trees. His thin arms ached, his back was sore, his hands bled, his nails were broken. But he kept on with the work. And at night after his supper of corn gruel or beans and tortillas he went to the schoolmaster's house and with sleep-heavy eyes studied the lessons he had missed.

Walking to the milpa with Dog in the dark early morning, he recited aloud what he had learned the night before. And sometimes during the day, when he rested from his cutting and lay on the mound, with Dog scampering about nearby, he would go over again the lessons he had learned. He carried a pencil and paper in his hunting bag, and sometimes, just for pleasure, he copied the strange carved pictures on the temple stones.

Little by little the studies became easier and his muscles hardened. Little by little the bush that remained to be cut became smaller and the fallen trees grew in number. And slowly as he chopped there came a feeling for the land. Each blow of his ax, each sharp machete thrust, bound him that much closer to the milpa—the old, old tie that had bound the men of his race through the centuries, now to this bit of bush, now to that, never the same field but always the corn and the land.

"*My* milpa," he said to Dog. "My corn." And in his thoughts he saw the field cleared, the arrowed plants thrusting through the soil, the growing stalks, the tasseled corn.

In February a boy child was born. He was named Juan Bautista (John the Baptist), for that was the name of the saint on whose day he was born. But from the beginning he was never called anything but Chan Tata (little father). He was such a serious baby. He looked around on his new family with wise, solemn eyes.

"Not like Tigre," Great-Grandmother said. "Tigre was the merry one. Always laughing and playing little jokes before he could walk."

Mother smiled at Tigre a little sadly. He is far from merry these days, she thought.

Now there is another mouth to feed, Tigre thought. Another depends on me. And he made his decision. He measured out more bush and cut down more trees. We will need more corn, he thought, to pay for clothing for Chan Tata and for Father's treatments.

"That will be our secret," he told Dog.

Not only would he plant more corn, he decided, but he would plant beans and squashes too, and chili peppers, to sell to their neighbors who planted only corn. Perhaps, he thought wildly, there will be enough so I can buy my gun.

He started to work eagerly on the new forest, and for a time his dreams so absorbed him that he scarcely felt the aching labor or the fierce sun on his back.

The day came at last when the last tree was down.

It had seemed to Tigre at the start that the cutting stretched out with no ending, the bush growing like magic almost as he cut it, as if the gods were jealous of man's leisure. But little by little, as small moments make up the seasons, so many ax blows, one after another, cut the bush down.

He sat down weakly and looked over the milpa, heaped with piles of brush and trees, some already drying in the sun.

"Ai!" he cried. "Ai!"

At home he only said quietly, "*Tzoki*—it is finished."

6. Study

The hot dry days sped by, each brilliant with sunlight. Tigre thought often of his milpa, of the piles of trees and brush drying slowly in the heat. Now the green will be turning to brown, he thought; now it will be turning to gray. The sun was preparing the land for fire.

Father remained in his hammock. His leg refused to heal. Infection had set in, and the wound would close over, then break open. Occasionally the medicine man came and made prayers and offerings and put healing bandages of anona leaves and honey and garlic on Father's leg.

Both Mother and Great-Grandmother felt that the hens and

honey spent for these visits were wasted. What could the medicine man do? Had not the stone and grains of corn told him it would be harvest time before Father was well?

"At harvest," Mother said, "Father will walk again."

"When the corn is in tassel," Great-Grandmother said, "the sickness will pass."

In the evenings Tigre went to Don Alfonso's house, though he had long before made up the lessons he had lost. The two had come to enjoy these hours together.

Tigre had always been a boy for asking questions. "Why does fire burn only the bush that is cut down and not the standing trees? Why is one part of the year dry and the other wet?"

And his family would answer, "Because it has always been that way. Because that is the way the world was planned."

But Don Alfonso encouraged the questions. He had an answer for each one, and sometimes he patiently drew the boy out with questions of his own.

"Why do you think fire does not burn live trees?" Don Alfonso said.

"Because of the sap?"

"Yes, Dionisio. If it takes so many weeks of hot sun to make felled trees dry enough for burning, living trees can resist and stop even strong milpa fire."

"Great-Grandmother says fire burns only the milpa and stops at the standing bush because that is the destiny of Fire—to burn the cornfields, not the bush. She says the gods of the bush protect the standing trees. Mamich says I am too curious, and it does not please the gods to be always asking questions."

"You should know better than that, Dionisio," Don Alfonso said. "Though in a way it is true. The good God in His wisdom protects the trees by giving them life-saving sap."

And the schoolmaster thought, Perhaps in the centuries gone by the boy's ancestors were among the great Maya princes and scholars, who alone possessed the highly prized learning and passed it down like hoarded treasure from father to son. The Spaniards destroyed the ancient collected wisdom by burning all the books of knowledge. But an almost inherited ability for learning persists in a few. There are always one or two above the others, with a passion and a quickness for study.

And he said, "Do not be afraid to ask questions, Dionisio. Never accept any statement without weighing it. Reason out the answer for yourself."

One day Tigre returned home from school to find his family in a great state of excitement.

"One of the hens is dead," Concha told him.

"Killed in the night," Mother said, "by a vampire bat."

"The door to the coop was left open," Great-Grandmother said.

Mother was sure she had closed the door.

Tigre tried to remember if the door had been open or closed when he left in the morning. But he had been in a hurry and if he noticed he had forgotten.

Mother was usually careful about closing the door. Most of their neighbors' chickens ran freely about the yards and road and slept at night in the trees. But Father, like one or two others, had built a small pen.

"Perhaps you did not close the door tightly enough," Father said.

"Be sure you put all the hens in tonight," Father told Mother that evening. "And be certain the door is fastened tight."

In the morning another chicken was dead. Great-Grandmother dressed it and roasted it with herbs and at dinner they ate the meat with a sauce of chili peppers.

"I cannot understand it," Mother said. "I closed the door carefully and fastened it with a stick."

The next morning two chickens were dead.

"Soon we will have no more hens," Great-Grandmother said. "No ceremonial fowl and no eggs to trade with the traveling merchant for cloth. Bad luck walks with us these days. First Father's sickness, and now the hens."

She took some tortillas and pozole and placed them on the altar at the end of the room before the Holy Cross.

"There must be a hole in the coop," Father said.

"There is no hole," Tigre said. "I looked carefully."

"It does not need to be a very big hole," Father said. "A crack merely. But truly a vampire bat cannot open doors and fly through wood."

"But why should a bat go inside?" Tigre asked, puzzled. "Are our chickens better than those of our neighbors? There are hens enough outside."

"Why does a vampire bat always go to the same mule night after night instead of going to a different mule so the first animal can make new blood and get well?" Great-Grandmother asked crossly. "Because it is a vampire bat. That is the way they do."

"There is nothing we can do," Mother said. "The gods wish to destroy us, that is plain."

After lunch Tigre went out to the chickenhouse. Again he went carefully over the coop, feeling it inch by inch with his fingers. There was no crack. He opened the door and crawled inside. A little later he came out. "Come here!" he called.

Mother and Great-Grandmother ran out of the kitchen. Father limped to the door.

In his hand Tigre had a vampire bat. "High in one corner, up under the roof. The bat was *inside* all the time. So," he said, "there *was* something we could do."

7. Burning Milpa

In March the Indians began to burn their milpas. All through the bush tall fires shot up and black columns of smoke rose to meet the sky. Smoke hung in low clouds over the village, at times shutting out the sun. The heat in the village was like an oven. And great winds roared every afternoon—the milpa winds to burn the cornfields.

The people went about their work calmly, choking in the smoke, blinking with reddened, smarting eyes. It was March weather, milpa weather.

The smoke and high winds excited Tigre, though other years he had taken them for granted. He was restless and could hardly keep his mind on his lessons.

One afternoon after school he went to one of the ancient

temples in the bush near the village and climbed the crumbling stones to the top of the pyramid. Below him the bush stretched out as far as he could see, waving treetops rolling endlessly to the horizon. Even the village and his home, so short a distance away, was only a narrow indentation in the deep. And here and there the surface of the bush was broken by the flames and gushing smoke of milpa fires. It reminded him of a picture in one of Don Alfonso's books, of a boat in a sea of waves, and long streamers of smoke blown backward by the wind from a thick black funnel.

He counted twenty-three fires toward the north and south and east. The sun was so bright he could not look long toward the west. But he thought there would be another eight or nine fires there.

His heart quickened.

Each column of smoke meant fire burning someone's cornfield, men working in the winds and flames. His field, too, was there in the bush below, waiting to be burned.

For a long time he stood there. Then he walked home slowly.

"I counted twenty-three burnings today," he told Father. "Everyone is burning. Petuch's father says the rains will come early this year."

"Perhaps," Father said. "The dry season began very early. It may be the rainy season will begin early too, though the Xoc Kinob, the Count of the Days, which foretells weather, says this will be a dry year."

Tigre waited, but as Father said nothing more he asked, "When shall I burn my—our milpa, Father?"

"Soon, Tigre. I have sent for your uncle. Today, by a traveling merchant, he sent us word. He will come on Saturday to help you with the burning."

Tigre's face fell. He turned away to hide his disappointment.

On Saturday he got up before daylight. He brought in the wood and gathered *ramón* leaves and helped Concha feed and water the goats. But seven o'clock, eight o'clock, passed, and his uncle did not come.

"He has been delayed," Mother said. "There is yet time. He will still come."

The hours went by. All day they waited, but Uncle Pedro did not come.

On Sunday the winds were high but the sky was cloudy.

"We cannot wait," Father said. "Any day the *manhache*—the strong March rain—will come. Do you think you can burn our field, Tigre?"

"Of course," Tigre said quickly.

Father put his hand on Tigre's shoulder and looked anxiously into his son's eyes. "It is a big work. You have the will, but the experience is lacking. It will not be easy. Remember to cut your burning stick from the *catzim* tree. Scatter your offering of pozole. Remember your whistle for the whirlwind, and stay back of the wind. The wind gods will help you," Father said.

Mother handed Tigre his hat. Her hands lingered as she hung his bag across his shoulder. "Be careful," she said.

Concha went with Tigre to the road. She waved as long as he was in sight. But Tigre did not look back.

When he reached the field the high winds of early morning

had died down. On the still air insects hummed. Yellow daisies, motionless as painted flowers between the brush hills, spotted the field.

Tigre stood at the edge of the milpa, looking at the piles of brush, brittle as matchwood—waiting, he thought, for his fire. His early-morning confidence died away. Suppose the winds did not hear his whistle? Or refused to answer his call?

Slowly he made his preparations. With hesitant fingers he cut his burning stick and frayed it at one end to catch and hold the fire. He scattered pozole.

"Save yourselves, tortoises," he called. Then, his heart beating madly, he lit the firestick and touched the first pile with fire.

The fire caught quickly. It crackled like rockets in the quiet air. Smoke drifted lazily upward from the brush. Tigre touched a second pile—a third.

Smoke was all around him now. He could not see the nearest brush heap or fallen tree. His eyes smarted, and he blinked back tears and fought to keep his eyes open against the heat and smoke.

He began to whistle, uncertainly at first, then stronger, surer— the Whistle of the Milpa, as his people had whistled it through the centuries, calling the wind gods to come and carry the fire.

Heat burned his face, his arms, his feet through the thin soles of his sandals. Smoke bit his throat and lungs. But he moved through the smoke, and moving always with him was the plaintive whistle, now rising in a fierce windy screaming, now slowing and dying away in a windlike sigh.

And the wind gods came. With a roar the winds swept down

upon the milpa. They picked up the flames and carried them running and leaping from pile to pile over the field.

Great joy filled Tigre. All through the bush, he thought, men are burning as I am burning.

He began to shout, his voice hoarse in the smoke-filled spaces. The winds had come. He had called them and they had come in answer to his whistle. He was working with fire and wind and with the gods.

An hour later the winds died down. The heat lessened, the smoke settled. Tigre looked over his milpa. A coarse gray ash lay over the field, with little flames still playing here and there. Here and there charred stumps of trees had survived the fire.

His eyelashes were singed. His face was burned, his clothing soiled, his shirt torn. But his heart was full. "A good burn," he said.

All the way home the knowledge was like a song. Mother saw him coming and ran to meet him. "Ai, Tigre!" she said. "Your face! Your clothes! Your hair!"

Tigre shrugged impatiently and went into the house.

Father gave him a long look of understanding. "A good burn, son?"

"A good burn," Tigre said.

8. Anticipation

The next day it rained. All day the rain fell, crashing on the bush and pounding on the thatch. It ran in streams from the slanting roofs of the houses and made rivers of the unpaved streets. It was the hard rain, the manhache—"the water the trees buy to start new leaves."

Tigre's family was all smiles.

"If we had waited for your uncle," Father said, "it would have been too late. We would have needed another two or three weeks of hot sun to dry out the field for burning."

A number of the men in the village had not yet burned their fields. They looked at Tigre, envy mixed with admiration, as he passed on his way to school. Several stopped him to congratulate him on his burning.

"They say I am lucky," Tigre told his parents. "I am a favorite with the Chacs (rain gods). We will have a good harvest, I think."

"I believe it," Mother said.

"Do not boast," Great-Grandmother said sternly. "When corn is not yet planted, how can you count ripe ears?"

Tigre was not worried. He felt capable of anything. The exaltation of the burning was still with him. Had not the wind gods come at his whistle? Had not the rain held off until his field was burned? The Chacs walked with him. They would see that the corn he planted grew ripe.

There was nothing to do now in the milpa until May, when the rains would begin in earnest. After the first rain had softened the ground for sowing, men would plant the seed.

In May, too, the village would have its fiesta for its patron santo's day. May third was the day of Holy Cross. Unfortunately the orchestra which went from village to village had been engaged to play elsewhere that day, but it would come on the fourth.

For three days there would be prayers and ceremonies in the church, feasting and dancing. People would come from all the villages around. And on the very last day there would be a *corrida,* a bullfight, for which the bulls would be rented or borrowed, and not killed. The older boys, many of them for the first time, would be *vaqueros,* leading the bulls into the bull ring. Already many of the boys were working on their ropes. At the dance the evening before the bullfight the ropes would be judged.

Tigre began to think about making a rope. "I too will make a rope," he said to Father.

"You are too young," Father started to say. Then he stopped. Had not Tigre already taken on a man's responsibilities? Who was he, Father, to say the boy should not enter the bull ring?

Great-Grandmother gave Tigre a shrewd look, and he felt as he always did that her sharp bright eyes were reading his thoughts, summing up all his faults. He had never been one to sit quietly and work with his fingers.

"I think we could arrange it," Great-Grandmother said to Father. "Only let it be a good rope, Tigre. Do not disgrace us with poor workmanship. And let it be finished if you begin."

Father bought the *sosquil* (henequen fiber) from two boys who came from another village to sell it. He paid for it with one of Mother's hens. All the fiber in the village was gone.

Tigre started his rope eagerly. He twisted the fiber and rolled it against his leg. But in a few days his excitement faded. The rough hemp cut his fingers and blistered his palms. In his awkwardness he tangled the cord frequently and had to undo it and begin again.

For several weeks he did not work on it at all. The high winds held, and the village boys were making kites. Tigre made one

too, though not so elaborate as some. He was in too much of a hurry to take advantage of the wind and get his kite in the air. Then the father of one of the boys bought a bat from a traveling merchant, and for a week everyone, men and boys, played ball.

The days were full of excitement.

One day a *yuc,* a very small deer, ran through the plaza, and men and boys ran after it with wild shouts until it was shot down.

Tigre was sorry afterward. He remembered the yuc's eyes and the way its heart pounded and its breath came in great panting sighs. The animal had had no chance at all It was different from hunting in the bush, where the deer had the protection of the Zip, the minor gods who watch over them. And each man got such a little piece of meat. Hardly worth the bother or the deer's pain. But during the few moments of the chase he had been as eager as anyone, his shouts as loud as the others'.

"How is your rope coming, Tigre?" Great-Grandmother asked slyly. "You have not forgotten, have you, that you asked to join the other boys in the bull ring?"

"It is coming," Tigre said. But he did not offer to show it. He had not worked on it for some time.

He determined to start again the next morning and keep at it until it was finished.

9. The Fiesta

April was dry. Every day was hotter than the day before. Gray dust settled on the houses and in the streets and clung to the shriveled leaves of the trees like swarms of tiny insects. The trees of the bush were only skeleton trees, gray bony trunks and limbs.

Everything gasped for water. Mother drew bucket after bucket of water from the well to give to her thirsty plants. They sucked in the water with a greedy gurgling, and in a little while the earth around them was cracked again and dry.

Father sat in his hammock or limped about the house and yard.

Tigre worked on his rope. Several times he had to unravel it and start again, but each time it was a little easier. A few months ago, he thought, he would have given it up as not worth the trouble. But his persistence in keeping on with the bushing had done something more for him besides getting down bush. As using his muscles constantly had strengthened his arms, so doing the hard thing had exercised and strengthened his will. It was easier now for him to stick to unpleasant things.

I am growing up, I think, Tigre said to himself. When two days went by without work on his rope he felt guilty.

Everyone was looking forward to May.

"Soon now the rains will come," people said to one another. "In May the Chacs will ride."

And Tigre thought, In May I will face the bulls in the corrida. In May I will sow my milpa.

Then it was May.

May third came, the day of Holy Cross. This was the day when the rains should begin. But from dawn to darkness the sun rode across a clear bright sky. The Chacs did not come.

The men of the village had cut down the trees for the bull ring the week before. They had built the ring, placing each tree a little apart from the next, so the people could look through at the fight. The church floor had been scrubbed, the altar newly painted. All the santos had been freshly painted and then dressed in fine, new, white cotton clothing. The dance platform too was ready, in the street before the church; and held up by four poles, one at each corner of the platform, was a covering of thatch to protect the dancers from the almost certain rain.

Every man in the village had a haircut and wore a red handkerchief about his neck. Every woman had a new hair ribbon and a new embroidered *huipil* freshly washed and ironed.

The fourth of May came, and visitors began to pour into the village. The bush trails were choked with travelers burdened like ants, bundles of clean clothing and hammocks on their backs.

The bulls arrived.

The orchestra came.

The village was jammed with people.

Every house had twenty or thirty sleeping at night in the room where four or five usually slept. The hammocks were strung like cobwebs, over and under one another. Men slept four and five in each hammock. Women sat up or slept with the children on the floor. The schoolhouse too was full. And many people slept in the open, hanging their hammocks from trees.

Tigre's Uncle Pedro and his family came, and Mother's mother and father and her sisters.

For three days the village was filled with music and laughter. Skyrockets exploded and spattered the sky with stars without pause. Every family had bought dozens. There was dancing and feasting and prayer.

The night of the last dance came. All the village was gathered around the platform—the men in their stiff white suits and silk shirts, the women wearing their gold fiesta jewelry, the girls as pretty as butterflies in their white dresses and little straw hats with gay ribbons and flowers. Holy Cross too had been carried out from the church, to watch the dancing.

The orchestra began the music for the dance of the vaqueros. The boys came on with their ropes. Tigre saw at once that his rope could not win. Some were so true, so beautiful, woven as smoothly as glass. But his was not the worst one either. There were others as rough and even more misshapen.

After the dance the boys went to the house of the fiesta leader. There must be no sleep for any of them during the night. This was the ceremony *vigil*, a test of their physical and mental endurance.

The next day they went together to the bull ring.

Ai! It was exciting.

The bulls bellowed and pawed the ground and ran at the boys and men with lowered horns. Pancho Noh had his shirt pierced, the horn just missing his shoulder. Felipe Dzul fell down and had to be dragged away quickly. Tigre jumped on top of one of the tree-posts of the bull ring just in time. One bull, poor thing, had

been through it all before. No matter how sharp the gaily deco-
rated barbs that stung his flesh, no matter how sudden and loud
the firecrackers exploding under his belly, he simply sat down
and refused to move and had to be taken away.

Outside around the bull ring the villagers watched and
shouted. "Bravo, Pancho! Bravo, Juan!"

Even Father was there, leaning on Uncle Pedro's shoulder.
Great-Grandmother stood straight and proud, never moving,
even when once the bull's horns came through the ring almost
in her face.

Concha's eyes shone. "Bravo, Tigre! Bravo, Tigre!" she yelled.

And Dog ran back and forth madly, making as loud a noise as
any.

Father tired easily, and he and Mother and Chan Tata left
early. But Great-Grandmother and Concha stayed until the
very end.

Then it was over. Tigre went home. Mother's father and
mother and the aunts and cousins had left. Mother had hot
chocolate for Tigre, and he sat in his hammock and drank it. He
was so tired he could hardly hold the bowl.

Great-Grandmother mentioned the rope. She was the only
one who did.

"You were too impatient," she said. "I watched you. Always in
a hurry to get it finished. But it was not the worst one," she added
kindly.

Tigre's head dropped lower over his chocolate. His eyes closed.
"Another time I will do better," he said sleepily.

"That I believe," Great-Grandmother said.

10. Planting

Now that the fiesta was over, the people began to think about the weather. Never had the rains held off so long before. Some of the younger men who had almanacs pored over their pages. The old men studied the sky and talked about dry years and muttered the dreaded words "famine" and "drought."

"It does not matter," Great-Grandmother said, "if the almanac says it will rain. Read the sky. The signs are not that way."

On the twelfth the sun was hidden but the day passed without rain. The fourteenth began cloudy. A heavy dampness lay over the bush and the village and penetrated the houses. "Surely it will rain today," people said. But later the clouds dried out and the sun broke through. The earth steamed, and at night the people slept with the doors to their houses open, to get relief from the heat.

The next day too was cloudy, and a little wind rose but dropped as suddenly as it had come. The clouds passed.

And then one night it rained. Tigre woke and heard it pounding on the roof. He lay listening. He knew Father was awake too. All night the water came down. Rain was softening the land to receive the seed. Weather was assisting man.

Tigre was up before daylight. He gulped down his atole. But even before he finished breakfast men were passing the house with their planting sticks, going to their milpas.

Great-Grandmother had Tigre's bag ready. Dog danced around, his small tail wagging frantically with excitement.

Father gave Tigre the planting stick and the bag of seed corn and some beans and squash seeds. "The Chacs have made the earth ready," he said. "Make a hole with your stick. Drop in the seed."

The village streets were full of hurrying men greeting one another gaily. There were men on the road, on the trails—a great surge of men, laughing and talking, each with his planting stick and bag of seed corn, each followed by his dog.

Others might bush or even burn one's milpa if it were necessary, but every man always did his own planting.

In the milpa the land that had been so dry and hard was wet and soft and compliant, waiting for the seed.

Tigre poked a hole with his stick in the rain-broken soil and dropped in a few grains of corn together with some beans and squash seeds. With the edge of his sandal he covered the hole with earth and stepped on it. Then he made a new hole farther on. Up and down he walked over the field, up and down, dropping his grains of corn in the land prepared by rain.

11. The Hetz Mek

That summer there was little rain. A week of hot sun would be followed by a few scattered showers that did little to relieve the land growing hard beneath the heat.

In June the first eager green shoots began to come up. Everyone was restless. Men stood in little groups about the streets or met at the schoolhouse, talking of weather and corn. Women watched with anxious eyes the diminishing piles of dried ears from the last harvest.

Sun and heat, a few light showers, sun and heat.

In June, Chan Tata was four months old, and on his month date the family performed the Hetz Mek ceremony for him, and he was carried across the hip for the first time.

Tigre caught the excitement of the household. Up till then Chan Tata was carried, if at all, across Mother's shoulder or arm. Now he would be carried, as all babies after the Hetz Mek are carried, across Mother's or Great-Grandmother's or even Concha's left hip.

"Is it always at four months?" Concha asked.

"Of course," Tigre said, feeling superior in his knowledge. "For a man child. Because there are four corners in the milpa."

"And for a girl?" she asked.

"For a girl Hetz Mek is made on her third month," Father said. "Why do you think?"

Concha smiled. "Because there are three stones in the *koben* (hearth)?"

"Yes, little daughter. Three stones. Three is woman's number. Four is for the man."

Concha helped to grind the corn for all the tortillas that would be eaten. In the long, flat, wooden tub in the yard under the roble tree Mother washed—Father's and Tigre's best white cotton suits, Concha's and Great-Grandmother's and Mother's finest embroidered huipils. She hung them on a line to dry in the sun, and later she ironed them with the heavy flat iron, heated on the hearth. Great-Grandmother killed and prepared the hens. Tigre carried firewood. There was work for everyone.

Mother's father and mother had been chosen as *padrinos* (godparents). They arrived about ten o'clock. It had taken them six hours to walk from their village. Everything was ready when they arrived. The table for the ceremony stood in the center of the room, and on the table were the nine objects that Chan Tata would need during his life—an ax, a machete, a book, a pencil, a prayer book, grains of corn, a pair of sandals, a planting stick, and a piece of money.

Tigre noticed that Grandfather had a new gun. Grandfather leaned it carelessly against the house outside. Tigre could hardly take his eyes from it. He always noticed men's guns. He knew each one and all its individual characteristics.

Grandfather had brought a new curva too, a present for Chan Tata, which he laid on the table with the other objects to take the place of Father's old machete-knife that was already there.

Then Chan Tata was brought in. Father carried him proudly on his arm, and everyone admired him. Grandmother had made him a new huipil for the occasion, made of softest white cotton and embroidered with little purple flowers and yellow deer.

Chan Tata looked solemnly about the room and held out his hands to Grandfather.

"Look! He knows what is expected of him," Mother and Great-Grandmother said.

"Here is the child," Father said. "So you may do him the favor of making Hetz Mek."

Grandfather took Chan Tata and put him across his hip, spreading out little Juan's legs. He began to walk around the table. He walked around once and picked up the ax and put it in Chan Tata's hands. "Here you have an ax," he said gravely, "so that you may learn to fell bush."

The second time he walked around the table he picked up the planting stick. "So that you may learn to plant seed."

He walked around the table nine times, each time picking up an object. "So that you may learn to read," Grandfather said, picking up the book. "So that you may learn to pray," he said, putting the prayer book in Chan Tata's hands.

Then Grandmother took the baby and walked around the table with him nine times, and each time she picked up a different object.

All through the ceremony little Juan Bautista looked solemnly first at Grandfather, then at Grandmother, his face puckered a little. Tigre was afraid Chan Tata would cry, but he did not.

Then it was over, and everyone was talking at once and laughing.

"Did you ever see such a good baby!" they said.

"He listened so carefully."

"As if he understood each word."

Mother laughed and caught Chan Tata to her and proudly spread his legs across her hip. "I am sure he understood," she said. "He is so solemn and so wise."

"Tigre was the merry one," Grandmother said.

"True," Mother said. "Tigre, my son, when we made Hetz Mek for you, you laughed the whole time, as if it were a game."

Great-Grandmother brought in the food and there was laughter and feasting. Everyone talked with mouths full. Happiness filled the house. For a while the heat and dryness were forgotten, and the worry about the corn. Surely tomorrow rain would come.

"I have forgotten something, I think," Grandfather said. "How could I be so forgetful!"

He left the house for a minute and returned carrying the gun. "For my grandson, Dionisio," he said and held the gun out to Tigre. "Because he who does a man's work should have a man's weapons as well."

There were cartridges too. And everyone looked at Tigre and laughed as he took the gun. They had all known about it all the time.

12. Drought

The dryness continued. There would be days of hot sun, then a few light rains that eased only for a little the thirsty land.

Tigre thought of the young corn in the fields and began to worry. He had always taken it for granted that corn grew ripe, that there would always be something to eat. Father worked and prepared the milpa and the gods sent rain.

Now he saw that man's work was not always enough. Sometimes in spite of all that man could do there was nothing. Weather was important too.

I can bush and burn, he thought. But if rains come before burning, the bush grows again and my labor is in vain. I cannot plant unless rain comes to soften the earth. And if rains do not come after sowing there will be no corn.

August came, and still the terrible heat continued. The days were hot and still; blue skies reflected as in a glass the burning glare of the sun. No one talked of anything but the weather, of the corn drying up in the fields. They were eating fewer tortillas now.

Great-Grandmother scarcely touched her food. "I have lived a long time," she said. "I have had my share."

Several times the sky clouded over, but winds came up and carried the clouds away, and with them the saving rain.

"The Sprinklers are angry," Great-Grandmother said. "Men are being punished because they no longer make all the old prayers and ceremonies the gods require."

Six more days went by without rain.

Everyone was burning candles to the santos, making offerings of tortillas and pozole to Holy Cross. There were services in the church, and prayers and chantings. All over the village, in every house, candles burned on little altars.

Mother and Great-Grandmother sacrificed a hen.

Nine days went by, and it did not rain. Ten days, and the rain did not come.

"The drought is a fever of the milpa," Great-Grandmother

said. "The land is being punished too because men forget the Chacs."

Twelve days passed, and there was no rain.

There was a *novenario* in the church, nine consecutive evenings of prayer to Holy Cross. The whole village was present, even the very old and sick. The altar blazed with candles, and men offered pozole and tortillas.

A little rain fell but not enough to save the threatened corn.

There were more prayers and offerings to other saints, and prayers to San Diego, imploring his protection from the drought.

But the drought persisted. Rain did not come. And at last the people turned to the old Maya gods.

"They talk of making the Chac Chac ceremony to bring the rain," Tigre told Father.

Father nodded. "It is time."

Father was much better now. He walked about the house and yard without limping and did odd jobs.

"How is the corn?" he asked Tigre.

"It is safe. But it needs the rain."

"Let them make the Chac Chac," Father said. "There is yet time."

Great-Grandmother was not so sure. She felt that the Chacs might think themselves so deeply wronged that they would not listen to men's prayers.

"Has it ever happened," Concha asked, "that rain did not come soon enough?"

"Often," Father said, "and times were very hard. But always in some parts of the land a little rain fell. People who had corn sold it at high prices to those who had money to buy. The very rich from other villages bought corn in the city, and men worked for corn. Many died. Some lived. And the next year rain fell."

"When I was a girl," Great-Grandmother said, "a drought was over all the land. Everywhere the sun poured down day after day and the harvests were lost. The old people and the very young died. Only the strong survived. Men killed songbirds and even the holy doves for food, and ate leaves and the bark of trees like deer. It happened in my memory."

Tigre watched her in fascination. She was so old he thought

the gods must have forgotten her and she would live forever. She must know everything that had ever happened, he thought. She was so shriveled that she was almost as tiny as his sister, and her hair was white, the only white hair he had ever seen.

"I remember it," Great-Grandmother said. "Sometimes it is very clear to me. Sometimes clouded. It was so long ago."

"What happened?" Concha asked.

"I went with my father and mother and many others to Chichen Itza to make sacrifices in the holy well there. The old people said that in former times boys and girls and jewels and chocolate and great treasures were thrown in the well in times of drought, as offerings to the rain god. In those old days in Chichen Itza they called him the Feathered Serpent, Kukulcan. And the Chacs forgave us and rain came."

"And the Chacs will forgive us now," Father said. "The rain will come."

13. Chac Chac

The whole village waited for the medicine man.

He arrived early in the morning and began at once to build an altar in a cleared space in the bush near the village. Every man and boy of the village was present except Father. His leg was healing but he was not yet strong enough to take an active part. And some felt, considering his accident, that he might be in disfavor with the Chacs. Tigre could represent his family. He was the lucky one.

At noon the altar, built on a table platform constructed of bush trees and vines, was finished. Not a nail was used.

Now the men went far into the bush to get the sacred water. No woman had ever visited the Rain Makers' Well. Only the Chacs had ever come here to fill their calabashes when they were preparing to water the corn. The entrance to the well was a dark narrow passage through rock. Following the medicine man, the men crawled like snakes through the opening. Each lowered his calabash and filled it with the holy water and crawled out. When the men returned in the late afternoon they hung the gourds above and beside the altar.

Hammocks began to swing beneath the trees, for now that the Rain Makers' water was on the altar no man must go home.

All through the night there were prayers and ceremonies, and all the next day prayers were offered to the gods. Sacred breads were offered on the altar. Men and boys went into the bush to hunt animals for sacrifice.

"You will kill two deer toward the west," the medicine man told them, looking in his stone, and the men went off, shouting. But later they returned, unsuccessful and anxious.

"The Zip protected the deer," the medicine man said. "Try once more." And again the men went off. This time they returned with one small deer.

The third day dawned hot and still and cloudless. *Balche* (a ceremonial drink) was offered, and hens were sacrificed, one hen from each man in the village. And now, after the days of preparation, the moment had come at last to implore the Chacs for rain.

Pedro's father was chosen to represent Kunku Chac, the leader of the rain gods. He was given a calabash, and a wooden knife to represent the *lelem* with which this Chac made lightning. Then he was carried to his station a little distance from the altar.

Four boys were chosen to be "frogs."

The medicine man looked into his stone and made his choices. One, Juan Cupul. Two, three, then four—"Dionisio Ku," he said.

Tigre trembled all over. The other frogs were older. He, Tigre, to be chosen too, to bring the rain! With the others, he knelt beneath the altar and was tied by his right foot to an altar post.

There was a great stillness.

The altar was no longer an altar. It was the world, and at each corner of the world a Being stood, not a village man but a Chac. All the gods of the bush and the corn gods were gathered unseen at the altar.

The medicine man knelt and began to pray, and men and boys knelt behind him, silent in the presence of the gods.

In the stillness the Kunku Chac rose to his feet and waved his lelem. He began to roar in a thunderous voice the Chac's thunder.

The frogs began to croak.

The medicine man prayed.

The thunder sounded.

The Kunku Chac waved his lightning.

The frogs croaked and croaked.

And in the heart, in the soul, of every man was the silent imploring prayer—Give us rain.

When it was over, Tigre went home. He could hardly lift his head for weariness and lack of sleep.

"How did it go?" Father asked anxiously.

"Truly, Father, it was wonderful. The medicine man chose Pedro's father as Kunku Chac. The thunder sounded and the lightning flashed. I was a frog. They say I am a favorite of the Chacs and Balams," Tigre said.

"Do not boast," Great-Grandmother said sternly. "If you are such a favorite, as you say, why is it the Chacs withhold rain from your milpa as from the others'? Tell me that."

"He does not mean it for boasting," Mother said. "It is an honor to be a frog. And when one is twelve. . . . The Chacs will understand."

"Now the rains will come. I feel it," Father said.

14. The Rains Come

The next day the sun and heat continued. Everyone watched the sky, looking toward the east, from where the Chacs would ride. But the sky was clear and glaring. The sun glittered like glass. The second day the sun still beat relentlessly down on the village.

On the third day, as Tigre was cutting firewood, he noticed a small cloud in the east. He watched it for a moment, almost afraid he had imagined it. But the cloud grew larger. He dropped his wood and started to run home, yelling through the village.

"Look!" he cried. "In the east! It comes!"

Everyone ran out, Mother and Great-Grandmother and Father, and Concha carrying Chan Tata on her hip. All over the village men and women and children came hurrying out of their houses, to stand in the yards and streets and point toward the east. The clouds spread, filling the sky. The sun was covered.

Some people were laughing, some crying. Boys and girls shouted, "The Chac! The Chac!"

Thunder sounded in the distance. Lightning broke through a cloud. Wind came up. Trees bent. A palm frond fell with a crash.

The Sprinklers were riding high and fast on their unseen horses, emptying their water gourds. The Kunku Chac rattled his thunder gourd and brandished his lightning over the bush.

Nearer came the rain. The people could hear it crashing in the distance on the bush. Nearer, nearer, pounding into the

parched cornfields, sweeping across the bush, driven by wind, came the rain.

"The Chacs!"

Then the rain fell. Like an avalanche, it landed on the thatched roofs of the houses. Mothers caught up small children and kissed them as they ran indoors. Boys shouted. Tears were running down Great-Grandmother's cheeks. Tigre stood in the yard and lifted up his face, feeling the rain on the corn.

15. Harvest

Late in September, Tigre and Father—and Dog—went together to the milpa. It was Father's first time.

The air was cool and fresh after the recent rains. The trees were crowded with new leaves. Flowers were everywhere— morning-glories in rainbow colors, yellow orchids caught in the tops of trees. Birds, bright-colored as flowers, sang gaily and flashed in and out among the green leaves.

Father and Tigre sang too as they pushed their way along the trail. All year long their work and thoughts and prayers had been pointed toward harvest. Tomorrow they would prepare the earth oven to make *pibil nal* (roasted ears). There would be tender green ears of corn to eat after the long months of eating only dried corn. They would offer the first cooked ears to Kunku Chac and to the Balams, and atole-of-new-corn to San Diego in the church.

They came to the milpa.

They stood without speaking, looking over the clearing. It was larger than Father had planned for. A bird of the milpa sang sweetly, to make the corn plants happy, and hopped from plant to plant. Yellow daisies carpeted the field. Beans grew on vines. Fat squashes hugged the ground.

And all about them, stalks drooping with their precious burdens, the corn grew ripe.

Glossary

ai! (ah-ee′), common Maya exclamation.

anona (ah-no′-nah), Sp., a tropical fruit tree; sometimes called *guanava;* the custard apple.

atole (ah-to′-lay), Maya, beverage made by boiling ground corn in water.

Balam (bah′-lam), Maya, corn god; generally used in the plural, *Balamob* (bah-lam-obe′), corn gods, also guardians of the villages. The suffix *ob* indicates the plural.

balche (bahl′-chay), Maya, a ceremonial drink made from honey and the bark of a tropical tree.

bravo! (brah′-vo), Sp., brave, well done!

calabaza (cal-lah-bah'-zah), Sp., gourd bottle made from a Yucatán variety of squash; a calabash.

catzim (cot-zeem'), Maya, a small spiny tree or shrub of the mimosa family. It is the tree from which the firesticks to start milpa fires are made.

ceiba (say'-bah), Sp., *yaxche* (yash-chay), Maya; a large tropical tree which has an important place in Maya mythology; the kapok tree.

Chac (chaak), Maya, rain god; often used in the plural.

Chac Chac (chaak chaak), Maya, name of the ceremony to bring rain.

chachalaca (cha-cha-lah'-cah), Maya, a bird whose cry is particularly noisy.

chan tata, Maya: *chan*–little; *tata*–father.

corrida (koh-rree'-dah), Sp., a bullfight; in Yucatán Indian villages a corrida generally means a bullfight in which the bulls are rented or borrowed for the occasion and are not killed.

curva (coor'-vah), Sp., a knife shorter than a machete with a curved blade; used by the Indians for cutting vines and small brush and bushes.

fiesta (fee-ess'-tah), Sp., religious festival.

guano (gwah'-no), Sp., a kind of palm tree; its large leaves are used to thatch the houses.

Hetz Mek, Maya, "to put astride the hip"; the ceremony in which a Maya baby is carried across the hip for the first time.

huipil (wee-peel'), Mex., native woman's dress.

iguana (ee-goo-ah'-nah), Sp., a large lizard.

koben (ko'-ben), Maya, hearth.

Kuilob Kaaxob (kueel'-obe kaash'-obe), Maya, minor gods of the bush and guardians of the trees. They are too numerous to have individual names and are always referred to in the plural.

Kukulcan (koo-kool-kahn'), Maya, the Feathered Serpent, the patron god of Chichen Itza; identified with the Mexican Plumed Serpent, Quetzalcoatl.

Kunku Chac (koon'-koo chaak), Maya, leader or chief of the rain gods.

lelem (lay'-lem), Maya, a machete carried by the Kunku Chac to make lightning.

machete (mah-cheh′-tay), Sp., a heavy, single-bladed knife about two feet long; used for cutting larger bush and small trees.

mamich (mah-meech′), Maya, "the little old grandmother"; term of endearment.

manhache (man-ha′-chay), Maya, literally, "water which the trees buy to start new leaves"; it is a strong hard rain that generally comes in late March.

masa (mah′-sah), Sp., dough made by boiling ground corn with water.

metate (meh-tah′-tay), Mex., a flat oblong stone used for grinding corn.

milpa (meel′-pah), Mex., a cornfield, either planted or unplanted.

novenario (no-vay-nah′-ree-o), Sp., a public religious service and offering, given on nine consecutive evenings.

on (own), Maya, avocado tree.

padrinos (pah-dree′-nos), Sp., godparents.

pibil nal (pee′-beel nal), Maya, roasted ears of corn.

pich (peech), Maya, a singing bird.

plaza (plah′-zah), Sp., public square.

pozole (po-soh′-lay), Maya, a drink made out of cornmeal and water.

ramón (rah-mone′), Sp., a Central American tree about twenty feet high; its leaves are used for fodder.

roble (ro′-blay), Sp., oak tree.

santo (sahn′-toe), Sp., saint, the image of a saint; in many Maya villages Holy Cross, an object of worship and religious rites from ancient Maya times, is also considered a santo.

sosquil (sos′-keel), Maya, henequen, the fiber of the agave plant.

tigre (tee′-gray), Sp., literally, tiger; in Yucatán and in Central America the word is used to mean "jaguar."

tortilla (tor-tee′-yah), Sp., round flat cake made of corn meal and baked on a griddle; Indian bread.

tzoki (tzoh′-kee), Maya, expression meaning "it is finished."

vaqueros (vah-kay′-ros), Sp., in Maya villages the young men who lead the bulls into the bull ring at the village corrida and who test their strength against the bulls.

vigil (vee-heel'), Sp., ceremony in which participants, who are vaqueros, must keep awake for a prolonged time.

Xoc Kinob (showk keen-obe'), Maya, "Count of the Days"—a system by which the Mayas check and countercheck weather changes for each day and hour of January, and, according to the results of this check, foretell the weather for the rest of the year. In Maya, "x" is always pronounced like "sh" in English.

xtabai (sh-tah'-buy), Maya, evil female spirit.

yuc (yook), Maya, a very small deer.

Zip (seep), Maya, minor gods who watch over the deer and protect them.

NEWBERY AWARD BOOKS
AND NEWBERY HONOR BOOKS
AVAILABLE IN PUFFIN